USBORNE

Usborne
A Sticker D
Castle

Zanna Davidson

Illustrated by Heather Burns
Cover illustration by Antonia Miller

Use the stickers to dress the Dolls on the 'Meet the Dolls' pages

Meet the Princess Dolls

Meera, Sophia and Olivia are the 'Princess Dolls'. They help the princesses who live on the Majestic Isle, with everything from new outfits to royal emergencies.

Sophia
loves books
and stories about
princesses of the past.
She is always calm in
a crisis. Her favourite
place in the world is
the palace library.

Use the stickers to   Dolls

Meera

is brilliant at making clothes
and jewellery. She is generous
and giving, and also likes
to follow royal rules.

Olivia

is a rebel princess.
She spends as much
time as she can outside.
She loves plants and
animals and is an
excellent horse rider.

Dolly Town

The Princess Dolls live in the Royal Palace, in Dolly Town, home to all the Dolls. The Dolls work in teams to help those in trouble and are the very best at what they do, whether that's fashion design, ice skating or puppy training. Each day brings with it an exciting new adventure…

The **Shooting Star** train whisks the Dolls away on their missions.

Madame Coco's **Costume Emporium** has everything the Dolls might need.

The Dolls love to celebrate at the **Cupcake Café.**

Rose Theatre

Animal Sanctuary

Bluebell Bookshop

Evergreen Sports Arena

Royal Palace
is home to the
Princess Dolls.

**Heartbeat
Dance Academy**

**Palm Tree
Film Studios**

**Fashion Design
Studio**

Mission Control Centre
lets the Dolls know
who's in trouble and
where to go.

**Pop Star
Stadium**

**Silver Sparkles
Skating Rink**

Honeysuckle Cottage

**Strawberry
Lane Stables**

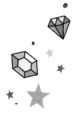

Chapter One

The Invitation

It was a cold day, and the Princess Dolls were gathered in the palace drawing room, enjoying some delicious hot tea and cake.

"Isn't the chocolate cake wonderful?" said Olivia. "I think it's Chef's best yet."

"We must let her know," said Meera, looking down at the last of the crumbs on her plate. "Sophia," she added, "you've hardly touched yours."

"Oh!" said Sophia, looking up from her book. "I've been too caught up with reading about the Majestic Isle. I'm so excited we've

been invited."

"Me too," said Meera, going over to the invitation on the mantelpiece.

The King and Queen would like to invite the **Princess Dolls** to the **Grand Welcome Ceremony** for their daughter, the Cloud Princess.

Time: 5pm   Place: Sky Castle, Cloud Kingdom, The Majestic Isle

"There's a map of the whole of the Majestic Isle in my book," said Sophia. "The Sky Castle is in the High Mountains, above the clouds."

The Majestic Isle

Ice Palace

River Kingdom

Frozen Lake

Lakeshore Gardens

Waterlily Palace

Shimmering Lake

Mangroves

Butterfly Fields

Acacia Avenue

Honey Grove

Palace Gardens

Wildflower Glade

Woodland Kingdom

"Wow!" said Olivia. "It looks amazing."

"It says here," Sophia went on, "that the Grand Welcome Ceremony is an ancient tradition to introduce the princess to her people. Apparently, the Cloud Princess is called Cora and she'll be performing a special dance."

"Now I'm even more excited about going!" said Meera.

I love watching dancing.

"And I can't wait to meet the Cloud Princess and see the Sky Castle," added Olivia.

"But first," said Sophia. "We'll need to collect our outfits. It's time to visit…"

"Madame Coco's Costume Emporium!" they all chanted together.

Chapter Two

Dresses and Tiaras

The Princess Dolls wrapped themselves up in their warm winter coats and hurried across Dolly Town, chatting excitedly as they went.

When they arrived at Madame Coco's, Sophia gazed up at the soaring building in wonder.

Madame Coco's EMPORIUM

Floor 9
Theatre costumes

Floor 8
Dance Outfits &
Accessories

Floor 7
Magical Dept. Floor

Floor 6
Royal Dept. Floor

Floor 5
Ballet Costumes &
Accessories

Floor 4
Pop Star &
Movie Star Outfits

Floor 3
Animal Rescue
Outfits & Equipment

Floor 2
Sports Cloth
Equipme

Floor
Horse Ridi
& Accessori

Ground
Weddings

Jasper, the lift attendant, was there to greet them, looking as smart as ever.

"Good day, Princess Dolls," he said, raising his cap.

Where would you like to go today?

"The Royal Department floor, please," said Olivia.

Jasper pressed the button and the famous glass elevator whizzed up and up before coming to a stop with a gentle

TING!

The Princess Dolls stepped
out into a huge room, filled with
dresses and glittering jewels.

"Oh! I do love it here!"
said Meera, clasping
her hands together.

"Ah! Princess Dolls,"
came a soft voice.

The Dolls turned to see Madame Coco gliding towards them. "I expect you've come for your outfits for the Grand Welcome Ceremony at the Sky Castle," she said. "I have them all ready for you."

"Oh, thank you," said Meera.

"It's such an important occasion, welcoming a new princess. We want to look our best."

"There's no need to worry," Madame Coco replied.

I've been planning your outfits ever since you first mentioned it.

"Sophia," Madame Coco went on. "I know how much you love stories of princesses from the past, so for you I've chosen a fairy tale outfit. A beautiful sunshine-yellow dress, lined with silk."

Next she turned to Meera. "I've dressed you in a rose pink sari," she said, "as I know how well the colour suits you. Its edges are trimmed with gold thread."

"And for you, Olivia – an outfit to suit your personality! A sparkling green dress, loose and floaty so you can feel free as air when you wear it."

Sophia's clothes

A beautiful sunshine-yellow dress, lined with silk, embroidered with silver leaves

Matching yellow shoes with blue details

Meera's clothes

A delicate golden hair slide

A golden, pink and red bangle

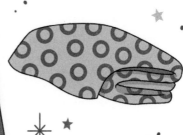

A rose-pink sari, its edges trimmed with gold thread

Embroidered dark-pink shoes (jutti)

Olivia's clothes

A sparkling green dress, loose and floaty

Green ballet pumps to match

"Thank you!" said the Dolls,
their faces lit up with excitement.
They stepped into the changing
rooms. When they stepped out...

But just then, the Princess Dolls' watches began to flash.

"Come in, Mission Control," said Sophia, tapping her watch. "All the Princess Dolls are here. What's happened?"

"Cora, the Cloud Princess, is in a panic," replied Mission Control. "She's anxious about the dance she has to do tonight."

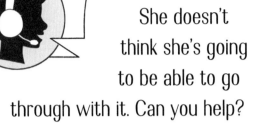

She doesn't think she's going to be able to go through with it. Can you help?

"Of course we'll help," said Olivia, determinedly. "We'll leave right away."

"Poor Cora! She must be so worried," said Sophia.

"Sending through the mission details now," said Mission Control.

Sophia pulled the screen from her bag, just as the mission details came through.

Mission to the Cloud Kingdom

Help Cora, the Cloud Princess, with her dance at the Grand Welcome Ceremony.

The ceremony will begin at 5pm.

It is a tradition for the Cloud Princess to perform a dance at this ceremony.

Cora is feeling extremely anxious and tearful. She says she can't get the dance right.

CORA THE CLOUD PRINCESS

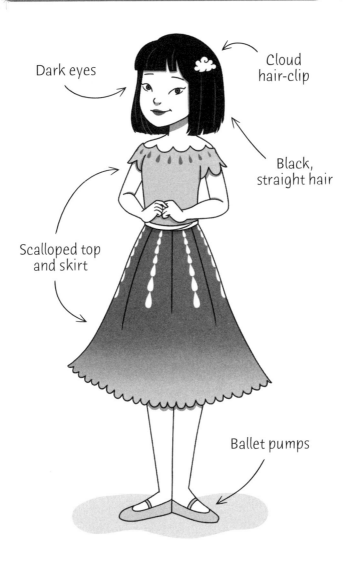

Dark eyes

Cloud hair-clip

Black, straight hair

Scalloped top and skirt

Ballet pumps

MISSION LOCATION:
Cloud Kingdom

Border of
Snow Kingdom

Cloud Pine Forest

Orabelle River

Border of
Woodland Kingdom

Sky Castle

N
W   E
S

Enter the Sky Castle
by the drawbridge
- Cora will be waiting
for you at the
Sky Gate on the
other side

High Mountains

Orabelle River

"No time to change out of our outfits!" said Sophia, turning to go.

"Don't forget your tiaras!" added Madame Coco, handing each of them a small sparkling case. "And take these cloaks, too. It will be cold in the High Mountains."

The Dolls
whooshed back
down in the lift

TING!

and stepped out
onto the street.
"Time to
catch the
Shooting Star
train," said
Sophia, tapping
the symbol on
her watch.

A moment later,
a train drew up beside them
in a cloud of glittering dust.

"Hello, Princess Dolls,"
said Sienna, the train driver.
"Where can I take you today?"

"The Sky Castle on the
Majestic Isle, please," said Olivia.

"Princess Cora needs our help."

"I'll have you there in no time," said Sienna.

As soon as the Dolls were on board, the train swept away. "It's mission go!" said Olivia. "Sky Castle, here we come…"

Chapter Three

Sky Castle

T he Princess Dolls gazed
through the window as the
Shooting Star train whizzed
through Dolly Town.

Then they entered a
dark tunnel, glittering with
hundreds of tiny stars.
With a
WHOOSH

the train shot out the other side...
"Oh! Look!" cried Sophia,
as they emerged from the
tunnel to dazzling blue skies.

"We're on the Majestic Isle."

"Hold tight," said Sienna, as the train began to wind its way east through the mountains. "We're going to have to climb to get to the Sky Castle!"

"Climb?" queried Meera.

But even as she spoke, the Shooting Star train was speeding through the air, spiralling around a tall, thin mountain, like a magical helter-skelter.

Below them, they could see the island, surrounded by a sparkling sea, and on either side, mountain peaks rose up majestically, their tops hidden among the clouds.

"Wow!" laughed Olivia. "I feel as if I'm on an enchanted rollercoaster ride!"

"We can see all over the Isle from up here," gasped Sophia.

As they climbed higher, they were enveloped in fluffy, marshmallow clouds.

"I can't wait to see the Sky Castle," said Sophia.

They didn't have to wait long. With a WHOOSH, the Shooting Star shot out from the clouds, and there it was – towering above them, its spires reaching up into the airy blue.

"Here you are, Princess Dolls," said Sienna.

"Thank you," said the Dolls, waving as the train sped away through the clouds.

"Isn't the Sky Castle beautiful?" said Sophia, gazing up at the creamy white walls and fluttering flags. "It looks like it's floating in the clouds."

As they walked across the drawbridge, Cora, the Cloud Princess, came running out to meet them.

"Oh!" she cried, her face pale and anxious. "I'm so glad you're here. I didn't know who else to ask for help."

"I'm glad you called us," said Meera. "Helping princesses is what we do."

But Cora was already hurrying back inside.

Please, come with me.

She led the Princess Dolls
through the grand hall into a
breathtaking ballroom.

"Everything's perfect," said Cora. "The sky chariots have left to collect the guests, the castle looks beautiful, I have my ballgown…but I just can't do the royal dance!"

"Why not?" asked Sophia, gently. "Do you feel you haven't practised enough?"

"It's not that," said Cora. "I'm just so *clumsy!*

I always have been. It's hard enough not tripping over my own feet, let alone remembering all the steps *and* doing the dance in my ballgown! I'm terrified I'm going to fall flat on my face."

"I'm sure that won't happen," said Sophia, soothingly.

"I really think it will," said Cora. "For hundreds of years, the Cloud Princess has performed this dance in front of everyone at the Grand Welcome Ceremony. My sister did it perfectly only last year! I can't see how I'm going to get out of it. What am I going to do?"

Chapter Four

The
Sky Song

Meera put her arm around Cora's shoulders.

"There's no need to panic," she said. "I'm sure it can't be that bad. Why don't you show us your dance?"

Cora nodded, still looking miserable.

She went over to the musicians and asked them to play her piece. Then she stepped onto the stage. Her first few steps were stiff and awkward.

"She's out of time with the music," whispered Meera.

Maybe she'll be better once she warms up...?

But a moment later, Cora tripped and stumbled. She didn't fall, but she stopped for a moment, looking lost.

"Oh dear," she said. "I've forgotten the next steps."

"It's an arabesque," whispered the violinist, "followed by a pirouette."

"Oh yes! Thank you!" said Cora. She raised one leg, twirled around, twirled again…only this time, she couldn't stop herself…and spun straight off the stage.

Luckily, the musicians
were there to catch her.

"See," said Cora, tears glistening in her eyes. "I'm HOPELESS."

By now, even the musicians were looking worried.

"This whole thing is going to be a disaster!" sobbed Cora. "I'm going to let down my parents…

I'm going to disappoint the entire kingdom. And it's all going to happen in less than an hour."

"There must be a way round this," said Sophia. Then her eyes lit up. "Hang on…I'm sure I remember reading about a Cloud Princess who did something different at her Welcome Ceremony."

"Oh!" cried Cora. "Really? What was it?"

"Hmm," said Sophia, "I can't remember exactly…"

Cora's face fell, but Sophia wasn't going to give up that easily. "Can you take us to the castle library?" she asked. "I'm sure I can find it in one of your history books."

"That's a brilliant idea!" said Cora.

She led them up the grand staircase, down a long, gilded corridor, to an oak-panelled room lined with beautiful books.

"There's a whole section here about tradition," said Cora, pointing to the far wall.

"Then let's start looking there," said Sophia.

She raced up the library steps, passing book after book to the others.

Soon, they were all frantically flicking through the pages.

"There's no mention of it here," said Olivia, putting back a copy of *The History of the Cloud Kingdom.* "Are you sure you remembered it right, Sophia?"

"I'm sure," said Sophia.

But then she caught sight of

her watch. "Oh no!" she realised.
"We're running out of time.
Only half an hour to go before
the guests arrive…"

"There's nothing here, Sophia,"
said Meera, putting down another
book. "Have you found anything in
your pile?" she asked Cora.

"Nothing," said Cora.

"Apparently there was a Cloud Princess who was so good she performed *two* dances, but that's not much help."

"Wait a moment," cried Sophia. "That book looks familiar."

She stood on tiptoes and pulled a dusty tome down from the top shelf. "I'm sure I've read a copy of this book before. This must be it…"

The others held their breath.

"Yes!" Sophia cried, nearly falling off the ladder in excitement. "I've found it! Look at this!"

PRINCESSES OF THE PAST

In 1840, at the Grand Welcome Ceremony for Cloud Princess Mei, the young princess chose to make a speech, instead of performing a dance.

"Could you do a speech?"
Meera asked Cora.

Cora shook her head. "I'm so
sorry," she said. "I don't mean
to be difficult, but I'd be nearly
as scared about making a speech as
I would be about dancing. And I
don't think there's enough time
for me to write one…"

This time, Olivia spoke up.
"If the tradition has been changed
once, to suit a princess nearly two
hundred years ago, I don't see why

it can't be changed again. What *do* you like doing, Cora?"

"I love to sing," Cora replied, almost in a whisper. "When I'm singing, I can forget about everyone else. I just lose myself in the song…"

Olivia smiled at her. "Would you mind doing a song for us now?" she asked.

"I've never sung in front of other people before…" said Cora. And for a moment, it looked as if she was going to be too shy to sing.

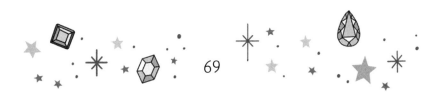

But then she took a deep breath and nodded. "I'll sing the Sky Song," she said. "It's the song of the Cloud Kingdom."

She closed her eyes, as if to block out everything around her... and started to sing.

Her voice soared through the castle. To Olivia, it sounded like flowing water. Meera thought of chiming bells. The Cloud Princess sang effortlessly, and as she did, her whole body relaxed. The Princess Dolls listened, spellbound.

Only when Cora had finished
did she open her eyes. The Princess
Dolls burst into applause.

"That was fantastic," said Sophia.

"Really?" asked Cora.

"You have no idea how good you
are," said Olivia.

It would be wonderful
if you could sing at
the ceremony.

"Are you sure?" said Cora, a faint smile spreading across her face.

"More than sure," said Sophia, firmly. "You have a beautiful voice."

"But my parents will never give permission," said Cora.

"Have they ever heard you sing before?" asked Meera.

"No, I don't think so…" Cora replied.

"We'll never know if we don't ask them," said Olivia. "Where are they now?"

"My mother's been away on a royal visit. She won't be back until just before the ceremony. But we could ask my father, the King. He'll be in the throne room. Oh!" she went on, clasping her hands together. "I do hope he says yes!"

Chapter Five

The Throne Room

The footmen opened the grand double doors to the throne room.

> The Princess Dolls and your daughter, Princess Cora.

The Princess Dolls entered and each gave a deep curtsy.

"Greetings," said the King, coming forward to meet them. "Cora told me she'd asked you to come early. I'm delighted to welcome you to our Cloud Kingdom."

"Thank you," said Olivia. "Your castle is beautiful."

"Is there anything I can do for you?" asked the King.

"Actually…" Olivia began. "There is something we would like to ask you – or rather, something Cora would like to ask you."

Olivia turned to Cora as she spoke, and smiled at her encouragingly.

"It's about the dance," Cora began. "I've been practising and practising, but I *still* can't get it right. I was wondering…if instead of dancing, I might be able to sing?"

"Cora," the King replied, sternly. "You know the dance is one of our traditions. You must do it!"

"I'm so sorry to interrupt, Your Majesty," said Sophia, coming forward. "But we found this book, and it seems the tradition has been broken before." She held out the book as she spoke. "It says there was a Cloud Princess who made a speech."

"If I can sing," Cora went on, "I won't let you down, I promise!"

But the King shook his head.

"I'm sorry," he said, "but this tradition is too important. And I know your mother feels the same. Your sister, Ling, never complained about it."

He paused for a moment, and looked at his daughter sternly.

"Cora, it's your *duty* to perform the dance. It's what is expected of you. It's what *we* expect of you... And I've never heard you sing before. It's very last-minute to be making such a big change to the ceremony."

"Yes, of course, I understand," Cora replied with a curtsy. But her voice quavered as she spoke, and the Princess Dolls could tell she

was doing everything she could
to hold back tears. "I'll go now
and do some more practice," she
added with a sniff. "Maybe it
will be okay…"

She turned to go, but Olivia
stepped forward. "Your Majesty,"
she said. "At least listen to Cora
sing before you make your decision.
I think when you've heard her,
you'll change your mind."

The King let out a sigh of frustration and it appeared he was going to refuse, but then he caught sight of Cora, looking at him pleadingly. "Go ahead, Cora," he said. "But I'm not making any promises."

"Thank you," said Cora, quietly. She knew this was her one chance. She took a deep breath, closed her eyes, and began.

The Princess Dolls could see how nervous she was. This time, her voice wobbled a little at the start, and it took longer before she began to relax.

But there was no
stopping the power
of her voice as
she sang of the
Sky Castle
and the
kingdom among
the clouds.

When Cora had finished, she looked up at her father.

"Well…?" asked Cora. For a moment, he said nothing.

"If I may," said Meera. "I am a huge admirer of traditions, but I can't think of a better way to introduce Cora to the Cloud Kingdom than for her to sing. She has such a beautiful voice."

The King turned towards them, then, and they saw his face was suffused with pride. "I agree," he said, smiling at his daughter. "I had no idea Cora was so talented."

He came over to Cora, and put his hand on her shoulder. "You have a wonderful singing voice," he said. "I'd love for you to sing at the ceremony... But if only your mother were here too. She loves our traditions. I just can't be sure she'd agree to this…"

"Please, Papa," begged Cora.

At last, the King nodded. "I give my permission," he said.

"Oh! Thank you!" cried Cora, and she wrapped her arms around him.

"I just hope your mother isn't disappointed," said the King.

Then he glanced out of the window.

"The guests are starting to arrive. Let's take our places in the Grand Ballroom."

As they all started to go, Meera noticed Cora hanging back. "What is it?" she asked.

"It's amazing that I get to sing," said Cora, fidgeting with her dress, "but I've never done anything like this before. What happens if I get stage fright and freeze?"

"I know you're going to be just fine," said Meera, calmly. "Take deep breaths. All you need to concentrate on is your singing. You can imagine it's just us again, with no one else watching."

"I'll try that," said Cora.

"Let me tell you a secret," Meera went on. "I often get nervous before events."

"But you seem like the perfect princess!" said Cora.

"I've learned not to let my nerves show. It helps not to think about yourself. After all, being a princess is about being there for other people, and doing your best."

"Thank you," said Cora. "That does help."

Cora hurried away to get ready,

while Meera smiled at the other Princess Dolls. "Time to join the guests," she said.

"But first…" said Sophia.

By the time the Dolls reached the ballroom, the guests were all chatting excitedly. The Dolls could hear the swish of silk across the polished floor and the room seemed to sparkle with everyone's jewels, from sapphire tiaras to ruby necklaces, to dresses studded with diamonds.

The Queen had arrived too, in a silk gown embellished with emeralds. Meera could see the King talking to her, and the Queen looking surprised.

"The King must be telling the Queen about Cora," Meera whispered to the others. "And I'm afraid she doesn't look very happy about it…"

"Welcome, everyone," said the King, stepping forward, "and thank you all for coming. We're delighted to introduce our daughter to you."

The King turned and gestured to the stage at the back of the room. "Please put your hands together for Cora, the Cloud Princess, who is going to sing for us all."

The crowd all looked at the
stage. The curtains parted…

"This is it!" said Sophia.

But the princess was nowhere
to be seen!

Chapter Six
The Grand Welcome

"Oh no!" whispered Sophia. "Maybe Cora has stage fright?"

But then came a gasp from the crowd. The Princess Dolls turned to see the windows of the ballroom being opened by two smartly-dressed footmen.

And there, flying
towards them, was Cora,
on a golden chariot pulled
by a flock of royal swans.

"Wow!" said Olivia, as the
chariot touched down on the
castle balcony. "Now that's
what I call an entrance."

Cora was dressed in a beautiful, sparkling gown, which billowed out in layers of silk on netting, its scalloped edges curved like a cloud. In her hair, she wore a rainbow tiara, set with rubies, sapphires, amethysts and emeralds.

Cora stepped out of the carriage and walked calmly into the ballroom. As soon as she reached the stage, the musicians began to play. Cora looked briefly at the Princess Dolls, smiled at them, then closed her eyes and began to sing.

If anything, this time her Sky
Song was even more magical than
before. The guests looked entranced
as Cora's voice filled the room,

soaring up to the ceiling,
full of power and feeling. The
Queen stared at her daughter,
her face frozen in shock.

When Cora finished, she opened her eyes, smiled at the crowd and gave a curtsy.

"Wasn't she brilliant?" said
Olivia, turning to the others.

"Even better than I could have
hoped," said Sophia, beaming.

Oh! I do hope the
Queen approves...

When they turned, they saw that the Queen was clapping hardest of all, her eyes glistening with happy tears. A moment later, Cora was beside them. "Thank you, all of you," she said. "You helped me be the best princess possible today. I couldn't have done it without you."

"It was our pleasure," said Meera. "You made us all proud! You sang beautifully."

"I'd better go and greet the other guests, now," said Cora. "I just wanted to thank you first."

They watched as she disappeared into the crowd, surrounded by a sea of people, all wanting to congratulate her.

"Oh!" said Sophia, excitedly.

"Over there – I can see the other princesses of the Majestic Isle. There's the Snow Princess, and the River Princess, and the Woodland Princess. Let's go and say hello."

The Princess Dolls mingled with the other guests and tasted the delicious food.

But as the sky turned an inky blue and the first stars came out, they knew it was time to go. They said their goodbyes to the King and Queen and waved to Cora, who hurried over to them.

"Oh!" said Cora. "Do you really have to leave?"

"We never know when we're going to be called on another mission," said Meera. "But we're so glad we could help you today."

"Do come to the Cloud Kingdom again," said Cora.

"We'd love to," said Sophia.
"It's a magical place."

They made their way through the castle, until they came to the drawbridge.

"Mission Control," said Sophia, tapping her watch. "Mission accomplished!"

"Congratulations, Princess Dolls," came the reply.

"And now," said Meera with a
sigh, "it's time to call the
Shooting Star train."

She pressed the symbol on her
watch, and they didn't have to

wait long before the Shooting Star
appeared, hovering beside them on
a shimmering cloud.

"Where to, Princess Dolls?"
asked Sienna.

"We should celebrate," said Olivia. "Take us to the Cupcake Café in Dolly Town, please."

They stepped aboard and the Shooting Star train swept away with a

WHOOSH!

streaking down through the clouds, around the mountain, leaving a glittering trail in its wake.

At the Cupcake Café, the Princess
Dolls took their favourite seats by
the window.

"What can I get you all?" asked
Maya, the café owner.

"Hot chocolates all round,
please," said Sophia, beaming.
"We're celebrating!"

"What a wonderful mission,"
said Olivia, once their drinks had
arrived. "I'm so glad Cora was
able to sing."

"And it was amazing to visit the Sky Castle," added Sophia.

"I hope we get to visit the Majestic Isle again soon," said Meera.

Then the Dolls laid out their hands, placing them one on top of the other.

Princess Dolls forever!

The End

Join the **Princess Dolls** on their next adventure in

Usborne
A Sticker Dolly Story
Ice Palace

with stickers

Zanna Davidson

Read on for a sneak peek…

"Mission Control here!" came a voice. "Are the Princess Dolls there?"

"We're all here," said Meera. "What's happening?"

"It's the Snow Princess on the Majestic Isle," replied Mission Control. "Her baby sister's

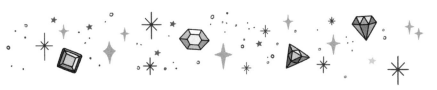

Naming Ceremony is today, and she's meant to be wearing the Ice Diamond tiara…but she's lost it."

Meera gasped and turned to the others.

"The Ice Diamond Tiara is famous – there's nothing else like it. It's made up of hundreds of

tiny shining diamonds and its centre is a beautiful blue diamond. It's been passed down from Snow Princess to Snow Princess for generations. It's even rumoured to have magical properties…"

"This tiara sounds very

precious indeed," said Sophia.

"The poor Snow Princess," added Olivia. "She must be so worried. We have to help her find it."

"I agree," said Meera. She tapped her screen. "Of course we'll help," she told Mission Control...

Edited by Lesley Sims and Stephanie King
Designed by Hannah Cobley

First published in 2021 by Usborne Publishing Ltd.,
Usborne House, 83-85 Saffron Hill, London EC1N 8RT, England.
usborne.com Copyright © 2021 Usborne Publishing Ltd. UKE